MILLY AND TILLY

The STORY of a TOWN MOUSE and a COUNTRY MOUSE

by KATE SUMMERS
illustrated by MAGGIE KNEEN

DUTTON CHILDREN'S BOOKS · NEW YORK

Text copyright © Kate Summers, 1996
Illustrations copyright © Maggie Kneen, 1996

CIP data is available.

First published in the United States 1997 by Dutton Children's Books,
a division of Penguin Books USA Inc.
375 Hudson Street, New York, New York 10014

Originally published in Great Britain 1996 by Orion Children's Books, London.

Printed in Italy
2 4 6 8 10 9 7 5 3 1

First American edition
ISBN 0-525-45801-8

Tilly was a mouse who lived in the country.
She was every bit a country mouse,
from the tops of her ears

to the tip of her tail.

Only the sharpest eyes could spot her home.
It was

down a lane,

near a meadow,

in the roots of a big, old tree.

Tilly was poor, but she worked hard to make her house comfortable. Each room was as neat as a pin and furnished with everything a simple mouse could want: a table, some chairs, and a soft little bed with a quilt she had sewn, stitch by stitch.

Every day Tilly got up early and did all her mousework before breakfast. She plumped the cushions, swept the floor, and even polished the stove.

Tilly spent most of her days gathering food.
It wasn't always easy finding enough to eat,
but at harvesttime there was plenty.

She picked grains from the fields,

cherries from the orchard,

and nuts along the hedgerow.

And, because she was a sensible mouse, Tilly filled her pantry with all these good things and stored them up for winter.

One sunny morning,
Tilly was out collecting
acorns when she bumped
into the mailmouse.
He had a letter for her!
It said:

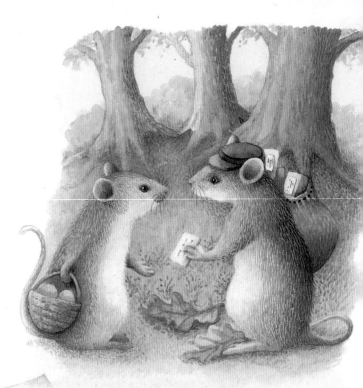

Dear Tilly,
I'm coming to see you
today. I've never been
to the country before so it
will be a big adventure!
love,
Milly.

Tilly was so excited that she hugged the
mailmouse. Then she told him all about Milly,
her friend from town.

"I hope you have enough food," he said. "Folks
say that town mice eat a lot."

When Tilly got home, she put on her apron and began cooking right away. She was a good cook, and soon delicious smells of baking floated from the kitchen.

After that, Tilly dusted the furniture again. (She had already done it once, that morning.) Then everything was ready.

Waiting was hard. Soon, Tilly began to worry.
What would they do all day?
Milly had often written about her life in town.
It sounded much more exciting than country life.
I hope she won't be bored, thought Tilly.

The clock ticked away.
One hour. Two hours.

Meanwhile Tilly kept peeping out the window
every few minutes. What if Milly had gotten lost?
Finally, as the clock struck six,
she heard a knock
at the door . . .
and there was
her friend on
the doorstep.

They kissed noses.

"At last!" Tilly squeaked. "I thought you'd never get here."

"I would have arrived sooner," explained Milly, "but a kindly snail carried my bags, and it's taken us all day long!"

Milly was hungry after her journey, so the two friends sat down to supper. They ate:

cabbage soup

roasted chestnuts

cherry turnovers

and

bread

seedcake

plum dumplings

and hot apple pie

Milly had a big appetite and finished every crumb.
"Do you have any cheese?" she asked hopefully.
"I'm afraid not," said Tilly.
Oh dear, no cheese! thought Milly. But she was
far too polite to complain.

That evening, the two friends stayed up talking
way past bedtime. Then, since she thoughtfully
had given Milly her bed,

Tilly curled up in a chair and went right to sleep.

But, in the bedroom, Milly lay awake for a long time. Nighttime in the country was so quiet that she couldn't sleep a wink.

And at dawn, when she was fast asleep, the birds woke her up with their singing.

After breakfast, the two friends went to the meadow to pick flowers. Tilly planned to show Milly how to make summer nectar.
"We'll need lots of buttercups and a bunch of daisies," she said.

While they were busy, a bee came along.
It buzzed all around Milly's head.

Bzzz!

Bzzz!

Milly had never seen a bee before.
"Go away!" she squealed. And ran.

On a different day, they went walking near the farm. Suddenly a sheep put its head through the fence and went

Baaa!

It frightened Milly all to pieces!

Tilly had tried her best to make Milly happy.
But before very long, Milly was ready to go back
to town.

"Come with me!" she said. "I live in a big house.
We'll have scrumptious meals every day. You'll
love it!"

Tilly had always wanted
to see where Milly lived.
So she put on her very best
hat and agreed to go to town.

They walked through fields and
over hills.

The sun went down, and the moon came up.

At last the friends reached town.

They scurried along a busy street

until Milly stopped outside a hole.
"In here!" she whispered,
disappearing into
the wall.

Tilly followed. It was all so strange that she felt
quite nervous.

Milly led the way along
a hall. The carpeting
tickled Tilly's feet.

Then they scampered
down a winding staircase.
Down around, and down
again to a room at
the very bottom.

And there in a corner stood
a dollhouse. It had painted
windows, a roof and two
chimneys, and a front door
with a real bell.
"We're home," said Milly.
"Won't you step inside?"

Milly showed Tilly all around her house.
There were lots of rooms, and each one was
beautifully furnished.

The green room was for sitting in,
and the red room was for dining.
The blue room was for afternoon tea.

Tilly peeped into the kitchen. It was full of
wonderful things, tiny pots, pans, spoons,
and dishes — everything a
mouse cook might want.
And best of all was a
shiny new stove
(the latest in town)
with knobs
that turned
on and off.

Then they went upstairs.

"This is your room, Tilly," said Milly. "I hope you like it."

The bedspread was primrose yellow, with curtains to match, tied with tassels and bows.

"Oh!" Tilly sighed. "How lovely."

There was a featherbed with lacy pillows, a dressing table, and a footstool. The wallpaper was covered with daisies that reminded Tilly of home. She peered into every nook and cupboard, her nose twitching with delight.

"Time to eat," Milly said.
"My tummy is grumbling."

Tilly supposed they would go to the kitchen,
                    but Milly laughed.
                    "Oh, I don't cook at all," she said.
                    "There's always food ready at the
                    Big House."
So the two friends scampered out of the dollhouse in search of some supper. Up the stairs
they went . . .

and into the
Big Kitchen.

"Here, give me your paw," said Milly
as they clambered up a shelf in the pantry.

Tilly gasped to see so much food. There were:

chocolate cupcakes,

cinnamon buns,

crusty pies,

nutty cookies,

jars of jelly,

a tray of tarts, and . . .

enormous chunks of CHEESE!

"Dig in!" said Milly. "Eat as much as you like."

But before they could nibble anything,
a cat came along,

jumped on a chair, and . . .

SPRANG!

The two mice leaped for their lives! They scuttled
along the baseboard, with the cat just a whisker behind.

"Help! Help!" squealed Tilly,
running like the wind.

"Faster!" squeaked Milly,
racing down a passageway.

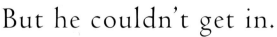

The cat pounced
and chased them
all the way back
to the dollhouse.
But he couldn't get in.

Once they were safe inside, Milly tried to comfort her friend. "You mustn't mind that old cat," she said. "He often tries to catch me, but I'm far too quick for him."

"Cat-and-mouse games are not for me," said Tilly, sniffling. She had begun to cry. "At least in the country, I enjoy my meals in peace!"

Milly had to agree. But she said, "I risk getting caught every day. But town life suits me best."

So the next morning, when the cat was napping, the two friends said good-bye.

"Write soon," said Tilly.

"I will," said Milly. "We'll always stay good friends."

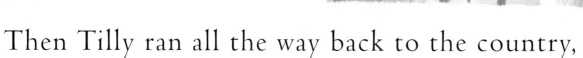

Then Tilly ran all the way back to the country,

made some hot chocolate, and settled down in her favorite chair to think about her adventures.